MW01141841

Extreme Animals

Nature's Slowest Animals

Frankie Stout

PowerKiDS
press

New York

For Nicholas Anthony Lazarus, a wonderful nephew

Published in 2008 by The Rosen Publishing Group, Inc.
29 East 21st Street, New York, NY 10010

First Edition

Editors: Jennifer Way and Nicole Pristash
Book Design: Greg Tucker
Photo Researcher: Nicole Pristash

Photo Credits: Cover, pp. 5, 7, 11, 12–13, 17, 19, 21 Shutterstock.com; pp. 9, 15 © SuperStock, Inc.

Library of Congress Cataloging-in-Publication Data

Stout, Frankie.
  Nature's slowest animals / Frankie Stout. — 1st ed.
     p. cm. — (Extreme animals)
  Includes index.
  ISBN 978-1-4042-4160-2 (library binding)
  1. Animals—Miscellanea—Juvenile literature. 2. Animal locomotion—Juvenile literature. I. Title.

  QL49.S796 2008
  590—dc22
                                    2007027482

Manufactured in the United States of America

Contents

Slow Can Be Good

Why are some animals slow and others fast? A fast animal can get its food by running after it very quickly. A slow animal, though, can use its lack of speed to **survive**. Being slow is an **advantage** that many animals use to stay alive.

Some animals move slowly so they can creep up on others that they want to eat. Then they kill their **prey** quickly. Other animals move slowly so they cannot be seen or found easily by others. This way, **predators** will not eat them. From snails to sloths, the world's slowest animals are crafty and surprising!

A snail has one foot. It pushes the snail forward by moving like a wave. Most land snails travel only 23 inches per hour (58 cm/h)!

Life in the Slow Lane

Animals need **energy** to live. Most animals get energy from food. Food turns to energy in an animal's body through a **process** called metabolism. A fast metabolism can turn food into energy quickly. A fast runner, like the cheetah, might have a fast metabolism. A slow animal, like the koala, has a slow metabolism.

The koala is one of the slowest animals there is. Koalas eat mostly leaves from eucalyptus trees. This food does not give koalas a lot of energy. Koalas can survive without using much energy, though, thanks to their slow metabolism.

Koala bears like to sleep during the day. They spend 75 percent of their time sleeping!

7

Slow and Furry

What if you lived in a forest and had brown fur? What if you moved so slowly that other animals could not see you moving at all? This is what slow lorises do. Slow lorises live in Asia. They sleep by day and hunt for food at night. Slow lorises eat plants, bugs, lizards, and other small animals.

Slow lorises catch their prey by moving very slowly through the trees. They use their strong fingers and toes to hang on to branches. Slow lorises can hang on a branch for hours! Once it is near its prey, a slow loris reaches out quickly to catch it.

The slow loris curls up into a tiny ball when it sleeps. If it is disturbed, it will make a loud buzzing sound.

Easy Does It

Sloths have legs that are made for climbing and hanging from trees. Sloths have long, hard claws on their toes to **grab** tree branches. Because of these long claws, sloths find it hard to walk on the ground. They are much better at hanging from a tree.

Sloths eat mostly at night. Even so, sloths spend most of their days and nights without moving at all! Sloths are hard to see because they stay very still most of the time. This way, they are not bothered by predators, like jaguars and eagles.

A sloth eats, drinks, and sleeps upside down. Because of this, its stomach is upside down, too!

11

Some sloths have three toes. These sloths are called three-toed sloths.

Big Eaters

Sloths have a large stomach. Their stomach holds a lot of food. Sloth's bodies take a long time to turn their food into energy.

Sloths

Extreme Facts

1. Two-toed sloths have two toes, instead of three.

2. Adult three-toed sloths weigh about 9 pounds (4 kg).

3. Adult two-toed sloths weigh about 17 pounds (8 kg).

4. All sloths live in forests in Central and South America.

5. Sloths have long brown and gray fur. Tiny plants called algae make their home on sloths' fur. Because of the algae, sometimes sloths look like they have greenish fur.

6. The word "sloth" comes from an old form of the English language. It means "something slow."

7. On cool days, sloths move more slowly than they do on hot days.

Gila Monsters

The Gila monster lives in the southwest United States and in Mexico. It is a brown and pink lizard. It is one of the slowest animals on Earth.

The Gila monster likes to spend most of its time in its burrow, or hole in the ground. It comes out of its burrow only to look for food. Because they are not very fast, Gila monsters cannot run after prey. Instead, Gila monsters creep up on animals such as mice, lizards, and worms. Then they grab their prey and eat it whole.

Gila monsters live in the desert, where it is very hot. To stay cool, they dig their burrows in wetter areas.

Slow and Fishy

Animals in the sea can move by swimming through the water. Many of these animals can move quickly, but one sea animal is not a fast swimmer at all. Sea horses are slow-moving fish that have a curved body.

The sea horse's body is best for floating or for staying in one place. Its curved, upright shape is not a good shape for swimming fast! Instead of chasing down their food, sea horses hang on to seaweed with their tail and wait for food to come to them.

A sea horse can change its color to hide from its enemies. Its skin can even have patterns like stripes or spots, like this sea horse does.

The Slowest Giants

Of all animals, the tortoise is well known as one of the slowest on Earth. There are many kinds of tortoises that live all over the world. One of the most **impressive** tortoises is the Galápagos tortoise. This tortoise lives on a group of islands near Ecuador. Galápagos tortoises are endangered, which means they are in danger of dying out.

Galápagos tortoises are big. They can measure 6 feet (2 m) across. They can weigh up to 570 pounds (260 kg). Giant Galápagos tortoises enjoy lying in the sun. They are also super slow. It can take one of these tortoises almost 6 hours to walk 1 mile (2 km). A person can walk that distance in about 20 minutes.

Since this tortoise is so slow, it has to guard itself. It is able to hide its head, arms, and legs completely under its shell!

Slow and Steady

The world's slowest animals use their body in special ways to stay alive. Though it might not look like it at first, being slow can be a good thing.

By moving very slowly, koalas can survive on only a little energy. Gila monsters and lorises use slow movements to creep up to prey. Animals that move slowly can be hard to see. Sloths, too, use this trick. They stay very still so predators cannot find them. All kinds of animals will wow you with their **extreme** ways. The slowest animals may be the most surprising of all.

Starfish move very slowly. They move by grabbing on to other things in the water, such as fish and seaweed.

Slow Facts

Speed of the Galápagos tortoise:
.17 miles per hour (.27 km/h).

Speed of the three-toed sloth:
.15 miles per hour (.24 km/h).

Speed of a garden snail:
.03 miles per hour (.05 km/h).

A person can walk 1 mile (2 km) in about 20 minutes. It takes a sloth almost 7 hours to walk the same distance. A snail takes over 30 hours to go that far!

Glossary

advantage (ud-VAN-tij) A benefit from something.

energy (EH-nur-jee) The power to work or to act.

extreme (ik-STREEM) Going past the expected or common. Extreme weather might be very hot or very cold.

grab (GRAB) To take with force or speed.

impressive (im-PREH-siv) Having a strong force on the mind or feelings.

predators (PREH-duh-terz) Animals that kill other animals for food.

prey (PRAY) An animal that is hunted by another animal for food.

process (PRAH-ses) A set of actions done in a certain order.

survive (sur-VYV) To live longer than, to stay living.

Index

Web Sites

Due to the changing nature of Internet links, PowerKids Press has developed an online list of Web sites related to the subject of this book. This site is updated regularly. Please use this link to access the list:
www.powerkidslinks.com/exan/slow/